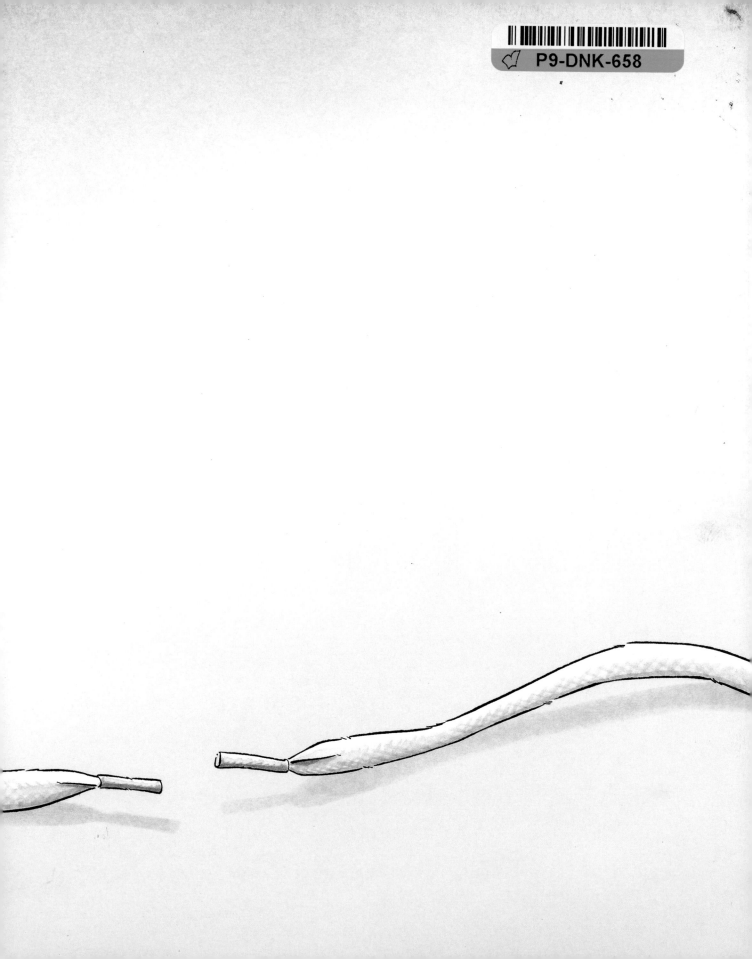

First American Edition 2004 by Kane/Miller Book Publishers
La Jolla, California

Originally published in 2002 in Germany under the title Was Benni alles kann
Copyright ©2002 by Lappan Verlag GmbH, D-26121 Oldenburg, Germany

All rights reserved. For information contact:
Kane/Miller Book Publishers
P.O. Box 8515
La Jolla, CA 92038-8515
www.kanemiller.com

Library of Congress Control Number: 2003109286

Printed and bound in China by Regent Publishing Services Ltd.
3 4 5 6 7 8 9 10

ISBN: 978-1-929132-60-7

Wilfried Gebhard

What Eddie Can Do

Kane/Miller
BOOK PUBLISHERS

"You need to tie your shoes,"
Eddie's mom tells him.

"I can't," Eddie says,
"I don't know how."

"I'll show you."

"I don't have time.
I have to go diving."

"Diving?" his mom asks,
"But...but..."

"I'm late," Eddie says.

Eddie dives down to the sunken ship.

He discovers the
secrets of dark caves.

He travels through outer space.

He explores the rain forest.

He tames tigers.

He flies with the birds.

He rides the prairie with great warriors.

He climbs the highest mountain in the world.

And then, he sees his friend Clara. She's in trouble.

Eddie must rescue her from the terrible double-tailed monster.

"Tie him up, quick!" Clara shouts.

"Uh oh," Eddie says to himself. "Tie him up?"

"Don't be afraid!" he shouts to Clara. "I'll be right back!"

Eddie runs to find his mom.

"Help," he shouts,
"I have to know how to
tie a monster to a tree!"

"A monster?"

"Yes, please,
show me, quick!"

"It's easy;
tying up monsters
is just like tying shoes."

His mom shows
Eddie how it's done.

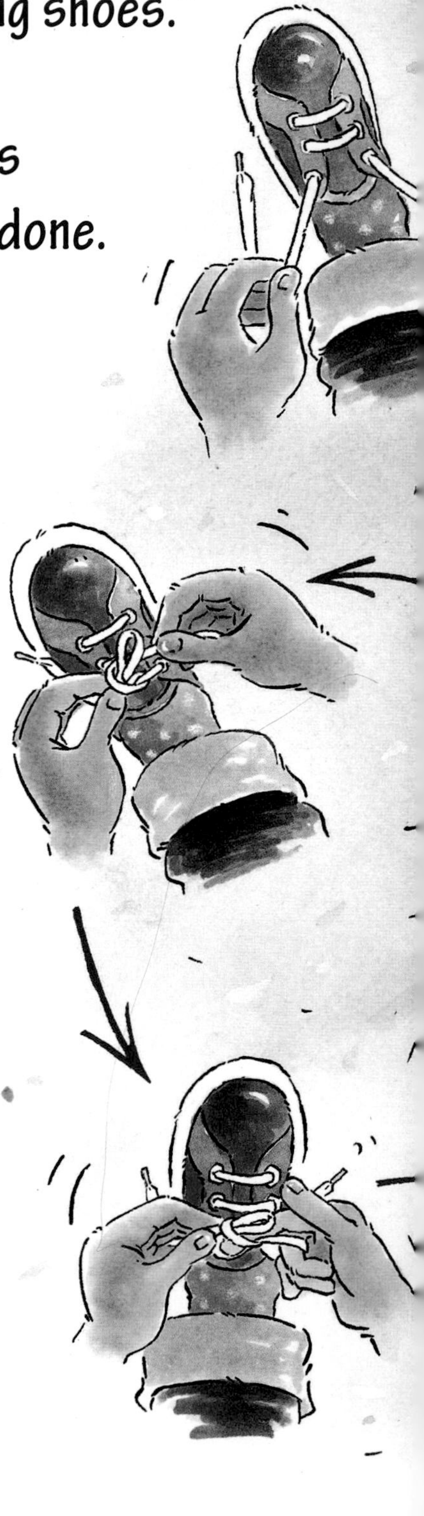

And then, Eddie does that, too!

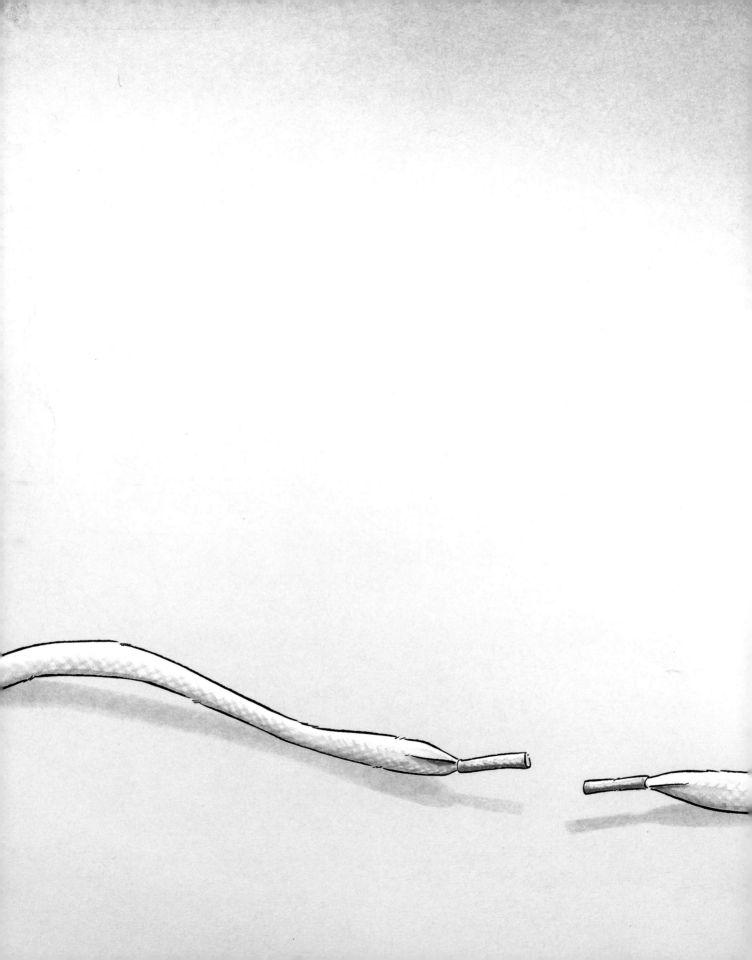